L. M.
Montgomery

Anne at Green Gables

D1136832

PENGUIN BOOKS

PENGUIN BOOKS

Published by the Penguin Group
Penguin Books Ltd, 27 Wrights Lane, London w8 5tz, England
Penguin Books USA Inc., 375 Hudson Street, New York, New York 10014, USA
Penguin Books Australia Ltd, Ringwood, Victoria, Australia
Penguin Books Canada Ltd, 10 Alcorn Avenue, Toronto, Ontario, Canada m4v 3b2
Penguin Books (NZ) Ltd, 182–190 Wairau Road, Auckland 10, New Zealand
Penguin Books Ltd, Registered Offices: Harmondsworth, Middlesex, England

First published in *Anne of Green Gables* by Harrap 1925
Published in Peacock Books 1964
Reprinted in Puffin Books 1977

This collection published in Penguin Books 1996
3 5 7 9 10 8 6 4 2

Set in 11.5/13.5pt Bembo Monotype
Typeset by Datix International Limited, Bungay, Suffolk
Printed in England by Clays Ltd, St Ives plc

Contents

A Tempest in the School Teapot

'WHAT a splendid day!' said Anne, drawing a long breath. 'Isn't it good just to be alive on a day like this? I pity the people who aren't born yet for missing it. They may have good days, of course, but they can never have this one. And it's splendider still to have such a lovely way to go to school by, isn't it?'

'It's a lot nicer than going round by the road; that is so dusty and hot,' said Diana practically, peeping into her dinner basket and mentally calculating if the three juicy, toothsome, raspberry tarts reposing there were divided among ten girls how many bites each girl would have.

The little girls of Avonlea school always pooled their lunches, and to eat three raspberry tarts all alone or even to share them only with one's best chum would have for ever and ever branded as 'awful mean' the girl who did it. And yet, when the tarts were divided among ten girls you just got enough to tantalize you.

The way Anne and Diana went to school *was* a pretty one. Anne thought those walks to and from school with Diana couldn't be improved upon even by imagination. Going around by the main road would have been so unromantic; but to go by Lovers' Lane and Willowmere and Violet Vale and the Birch Path was romantic, if ever anything was.

Lovers' Lane opened out below the orchard at Green Gables and stretched far up into the woods to the end of the Cuthbert Farm. It was the way by which the cows were taken to the back pasture and the wood hauled home in winter. Anne had named it Lovers' Lane before she had been a month at Green Gables.

'Not that lovers ever really walk there,' she explained to Marilla, 'but Diana and I are reading a perfectly magnificent book and there's a Lovers' Lane in it. So we want to have one, too. And it's a very pretty name, don't you think? So romantic! We can imagine the lovers into it, you know. I like that lane because you can think out loud there without people calling you crazy.'

Anne, starting out alone in the morning, went down Lovers' Lane as far as the brook. Here Diana met her, and the two little girls went on up the lane under the leafy arch of maples – 'maples are such sociable trees,' said Anne; 'they're always rustling and whispering to you,' – until they came to a rustic bridge. Then they left the lane and walked through Mr Barry's back field and past Willowmere. Beyond Willowmere came Violet Vale – a little green dimple in the shadow of Mr Andrew Bell's big woods. 'Of course there are no violets there now,' Anne told Marilla, 'but Diana says there are millions of them in spring. Oh, Marilla, can't you just imagine you see them? It actually takes away my breath. I named it Violet Vale. Diana says she never saw the beat of me for hitting on fancy names for places. It's nice to be clever at something, isn't it? But Diana named the Birch Path. She wanted to, so I let her; but I'm sure I could have found something more poetical than plain Birch Path. Anybody can think of a name like that. But the Birch Path is one of the prettiest places in the world, Marilla.'

It was. Other people besides Anne thought so when they stumbled on it. It was a little narrow, twisting path, winding down over a long hill straight through Mr Bell's woods, where the light came down sifted through so many emerald screens that it was as flawless as the heart of a diamond. It was 3 fringed in all its length with slim young birches, white-stemmed and lissom-boughed; ferns and star-flowers and wild lilies of the valley and scarlet tufts of pigeon berries grew thickly along it; and always there was a delightful spiciness in the air and music of bird calls and the murmur and laugh of wood winds in the trees overhead. Now and then you might see a rabbit skipping across the road if you were quiet – which, with Anne and Diana, happened about once in a blue moon. Down in the valley the path came out to the main road and then it was just up the spruce hill to the school.

The Avonlea school was a whitewashed building low in the eaves and wide in the windows, furnished inside with comfortable substantial old-fashioned desks that opened and shut, and were carved all over their lids with the initials and hieroglyphics of three generations of school-children. The schoolhouse was set back from the road and behind it was a dusky fir wood and a brook where all the children put their bottles of milk in the morning to keep cool and sweet until dinner hour.

Marilla had seen Anne start off to school on the first day of September with many secret misgivings.

Anne was such an odd girl. How would she get on with the other children? And how on earth would she ever manage to hold her tongue during school hours?

Things went better than Marilla feared, however. Anne came home that evening in high spirits.

'I think I'm going to like school here,' she announced. 'I don't think much of the master, though. He's all the time curling his moustache and making eyes at Prissy Andrews. Prissy is grown-up, you know. She's sixteen and she's studying for the entrance examination into Queen's Academy at Charlottetown next year. Tillie Boulter says the master is *dead gone* on her. She's got a beautiful complexion and curly brown hair and she does it up so elegantly. She sits in the long seat at the back and he sits there, too, most of the time – to explain her lessons, he says. But Ruby Gillis says she saw him writing something on her slate and when Prissy read it she blushed as red as a beet and giggled; and Ruby Gillis says she doesn't believe it had anything to do with the lesson.'

'Anne Shirley, don't let me hear you talking about your teacher in that way again,' said Marilla sharply. 5

'You don't go to school to criticize the master. I guess he can teach *you* something and it's your business to learn. And I want you to understand right off that you are not to come home telling tales about him. That is something I won't encourage. I hope you were a good girl.'

'Indeed I was,' said Anne comfortably. 'It wasn't so hard as you might imagine, either. I sit with Diana. Our seat is right by the window and we can look down to the Lake of Shining Waters. There are a lot of nice girls in school and we had scrumptious fun playing at dinner-time. It's so nice to have a lot of little girls to play with. But of course I like Diana best and always will. I *adore* Diana. I'm dreadfully far behind the others. They're all in the fifth book and I'm only in the fourth. I feel that it's a kind of a disgrace. But there's not one of them has such an imagination as I have, and I soon found that out. We had reading and geography and Canadian History and dictation today. Mr Phillips said my spelling was disgraceful and he held up my slate so that everybody could see it, all marked over. I felt so mortified, Marilla; he might have been politer to a stranger, I think. Ruby Gillis gave me an apple and Sophia

Sloane lent me a lovely pink card with "May I see you home?" on it. I'm to give it back to her tomorrow. And Tillie Boulter let me wear her bead ring all the afternoon. Can I have some of those pearl beads off the old pincushion in the garret to make myself a ring? And oh, Marilla, Jane Andrews told me that Minnie MacPherson told her that she heard Prissy Andrews tell Sara Gillis that I had a very pretty nose. Marilla, that is the first compliment I have ever had in my life and you can't imagine what a strange feeling it gave me. Marilla, have I really a pretty nose? I know you'll tell me the truth.'

'Your nose is well enough,' said Marilla shortly. Secretly she thought Anne's nose was a remarkably pretty one; but she had no intention of telling her so.

That was three weeks ago and all had gone smoothly so far. And now, this crisp September morning, Anne and Diana were tripping blithely down the Birch Path, two of the happiest little girls in Avonlea.

'I guess Gilbert Blythe will be in school today,' said Diana. 'He's been visiting his cousins over in New Brunswick all summer and he only came home Saturday night. He's *awf'ly* handsome, Anne. And he 7 teases the girls something terrible. He just torments our lives out.'

Diana's voice indicated that she rather liked having her life tormented out than not.

'Gilbert Blythe?' said Anne. 'Isn't it his name that's written up on the porch wall with Julia Bell's and a big "Take Notice" over them?'

'Yes,' said Diana, tossing her head, 'but I'm sure he doesn't like Julia Bell so very much. I've heard him say he studied the multiplication table by her freckles.'

'Oh, don't speak about freckles to me,' implored Anne. 'It isn't delicate when I've got so many. But I do think that writing take-notices up on the wall about the boys and girls is the silliest ever. I should just like to see anybody dare to write my name up with a boy's. Not, of course,' she hastened to add, 'that anybody would.'

Anne sighed. She didn't want her name written up. But it was a little humiliating to know that there was no danger of it.

'Nonsense,' said Diana, whose black eyes and glossy tresses had played such havoc with the hearts of Avonlea schoolboys that her name figured on the porch walls in half a dozen take-notices. 'It's only meant as a joke. And don't you be too sure your name won't ever be written up. Charlie Sloane is *dead gone* on you. He told his mother – his *mother*, mind you – that you were the smartest girl in school. That's better than being good-looking.'

'No, it isn't,' said Anne, feminine to the core. 'I'd rather be pretty than clever. And I hate Charlie Sloane. I can't bear a boy with goggle eyes. If anyone wrote my name up with his I'd *never* get over it, Diana Barry. But it *is* nice to keep head of your class.'

'You'll have Gilbert in your class after this,' said Diana, 'and he's used to being head of his class, I can tell you. He's only in the fourth book although he's nearly fourteen. Four years ago his father was sick and had to go out to Alberta for his health and Gilbert went with him. They were there three years and Gil didn't go to school hardly any until they came back. You won't find it so easy to keep head after this, Anne.'

'I'm glad,' said Anne quickly. 'I couldn't really feel proud of keeping head of little boys and girls of just nine or ten. I got up yesterday spelling "ebullition". 9

Josie Pye was head and, mind you, she peeped in her book. Mr Phillips didn't see her – he was looking at Prissy Andrews – but I did. I just swept her a look of freezing scorn and she got as red as a beet and spelled it wrong after all.'

'Those Pye girls are cheats all round,' said Diana indignantly, as they climbed the fence of the main road. 'Gertie Pye actually went and put her milk bottle in my place in the brook yesterday. Did you ever? I don't speak to her now.'

When Mr Phillips was in the back of the room hearing Prissy Andrews's Latin, Diana whispered to Anne:

'That's Gilbert Blythe sitting right across the aisle from you, Anne. Just look at him and see if you don't think he's handsome.'

Anne looked accordingly. She had a good chance to do so, for the said Gilbert Blythe was absorbed in stealthily pinning the long yellow braid of Ruby Gillis, who sat in front of him, to the back of her seat. He was a tall boy, with curly brown hair, roguish hazel eyes, and a mouth twisted into a teasing smile. Presently Ruby Gillis started up to take a sum to the master; she fell back into her seat with a little shriek, believing that her hair was pulled out by the roots. Everybody looked at her and Mr Phillips glared so sternly that Ruby began to cry. Gilbert had whisked the pin out of sight and was studying his history with the soberest face in the world; but when the commotion subsided he looked at Anne and winked with inexpressible drollery.

'I think your Gilbert Blythe *is* handsome,' confided Anne to Diana, 'but I think he's very bold. It isn't good manners to wink at a strange girl.'

But it was not until the afternoon that things really began to happen.

Mr Phillips was back in the corner explaining a problem in algebra to Prissy Andrews and the rest of the scholars were doing pretty much as they pleased, eating green apples, whispering, drawing pictures on their slates, and driving crickets, harnessed to strings, up and down the aisle. Gilbert Blythe was trying to make Anne Shirley look at him and failing utterly, because Anne was at that moment totally oblivious, not only of the very existence of Gilbert Blythe, but of every other scholar in Avonlea school and of Avonlea school itself. With her chin propped on her 11 hands and her eyes fixed on the blue glimpse of the Lake of Shining Waters that the west window afforded, she was far away in a gorgeous dreamland, hearing and seeing nothing save her own wonderful visions.

Gilbert Blythe wasn't used to putting himself out to make a girl look at him and meeting with failure. She *should* look at him, that red-haired Shirley girl with the little pointed chin and big eyes that weren't like the eyes of any other girl in Avonlea school.

Gilbert reached across the aisle, picked up the end of Anne's long red braid, held it out at arm's length, and said in a piercing whisper:

'Carrots! Carrots!'

Then Anne looked at him with a vengeance!

She did more than look. She sprang to her feet, her bright fancies fallen into cureless ruin. She flashed one indignant glance at Gilbert from eyes whose angry sparkle was swiftly quenched in equally angry tears.

'You mean, hateful boy!' she exclaimed passionately. 'How dare you!'

And then – Thwack! Anne had brought her slate

down on Gilbert's head and cracked it – slate, not head – clear across.

Avonlea school always enjoyed a scene. This was an especially enjoyable one. Everybody said, 'Oh,' in horrified delight. Diana gasped. Ruby Gillis, who was inclined to be hysterical, began to cry. Tommy Sloane let his team of crickets escape him altogether while he stared open-mouthed at the tableau.

Mr Phillips stalked down the aisle and laid his hand heavily on Anne's shoulder.

'Anne Shirley, what does this mean?' he said angrily.

Anne returned no answer. It was asking too much of flesh and blood to expect her to tell before the whole school that she had been called 'carrots'. Gilbert it was who spoke up stoutly.

'It was my fault, Mr Phillips. I teased her.'

Mr Phillips paid no heed to Gilbert.

'I am sorry to see a pupil of mine displaying such a temper and such a vindictive spirit,' he said in a solemn tone, as if the mere fact of being a pupil of his ought to root out all evil passions from the hearts of small imperfect mortals. 'Anne, go and stand on the 13 platform in front of the blackboard for the rest of the afternoon.'

Anne would have infinitely preferred a whipping to this punishment, under which her sensitive spirit quivered as from a whiplash. With a white, set face she obeyed. Mr Phillips took a chalk crayon and wrote on the blackboard above her head:

'Ann Shirley has a very bad temper. Ann Shirley must learn to control her temper,' and then read it out loud, so that even the primer class, who couldn't read writing, should understand it.

Anne stood there the rest of the afternoon with that legend above her. She did not cry or hang her head. Anger was still too hot in her heart for that and it sustained her amid all her agony of humiliation. With resentful eyes and passion-red cheeks she confronted alike Diana's sympathetic gaze and Charlie Sloane's indignant nods and Josie Pye's malicious smiles. As for Gilbert Blythe, she would not even look at him. She would *never* look at him again! She would never speak to him! !

When school was dismissed Anne marched out with her red head held high. Gilbert Blythe tried to
14   intercept her at the porch door.

'I'm awfully sorry I made fun of your hair, Anne,' he whispered contritely. 'Honest I am. Don't be mad for keeps, now.'

Anne swept by disdainfully, without look or sign of hearing. 'Oh, how could you, Anne?' breathed Diana as they went down the road, half reproachfully, half admiringly. Diana felt that *she* could never have resisted Gilbert's plea.

'I shall never forgive Gilbert Blythe,' said Anne firmly. 'And Mr Phillips spelled my name without an *e* too. The iron has entered into my soul, Diana.'

Diana hadn't the least idea what Anne meant, but she understood it was something terrible.

'You mustn't mind Gilbert making fun of your hair,' she said soothingly. 'Why, he makes fun of all girls. He laughs at mine because it's so black. He's called me a crow a dozen times; and I never heard him apologize for anything before either.'

'There's a great deal of difference between being called a crow and being called carrots,' said Anne with dignity. 'Gilbert Blythe has hurt my feelings *excruciatingly*, Diana.'

It is possible the matter might have blown over without more excruciation if nothing else had 15 happened. But when things begin to happen they are apt to keep on.

Avonlea scholars often spent noon hour picking gum in Mr Bell's spruce grove over the hill and across his big pasture field. From there they could keep an eye on Eben Wright's house, where the master boarded. When they saw Mr Phillips emerging therefrom they ran for the schoolhouse; but the distance being about three times longer than Mr Wright's lane they were very apt to arrive there, breathless and gasping, some three minutes too late.

On the following day Mr Phillips was seized with one of his spasmodic fits of reform and announced, before going to dinner, that he should expect to find all the scholars in their seats when he returned. Anyone who came in late would be punished.

All the boys and some of the girls went to Mr Bell's spruce grove as usual, fully intending to stay only long enough to 'pick a chew'. But spruce groves are seductive and yellow nuts of gum beguiling; they picked and loitered and strayed; and as usual the first thing that recalled them to a sense of the flight of time was Jimmy Glover shouting from the top of a patriarchal old spruce, 'Master's coming.'

The girls, who were on the ground, started first and managed to reach the schoolhouse in time, but without a second to spare. The boys, who had to wriggle hastily down from the trees, were later; and Anne, who had not been picking gum at all but was wandering happily in the far end of the grove, waist deep among the bracken, singing softly to herself, with a wreath of rice lilies on her hair as if she were some wild divinity of the shadowy places, was latest of all. Anne could run like a deer, however; run she did with the impish result that she overtook the boys at the door and was swept into the schoolhouse among them just as Mr Phillips was in the act of hanging up his hat.

Mr Phillips's brief reforming energy was over; he didn't want the bother of punishing a dozen pupils; but it was necessary to do something to save his word, so he looked about for a scapegoat and found it in Anne, who had dropped into her seat, gasping for breath, with her forgotten lily wreath hanging askew over one ear and giving her a particularly rakish and dishevelled appearance.

'Anne Shirley, since you seem to be so fond of the boys' company we shall indulge your taste for it this afternoon,' he said sarcastically. 'Take those flowers out of your hair and sit with Gilbert Blythe.'

The other boys snickered. Diana, turning pale with pity, plucked the wreath from Anne's hair and squeezed her hand. Anne stared at the master as if turned to stone.

'Did you hear what I said, Anne?' queried Mr Phillips sternly.

'Yes, sir,' said Anne slowly, 'but I didn't suppose you really meant it.'

'I assure you I did' – still with the sarcastic inflection which all the children, and Anne especially, hated. It flicked on the raw. 'Obey me at once.'

For a moment Anne looked as if she meant to disobey. Then, realizing that there was no help for it, she rose haughtily, stepped across the aisle, sat down beside Gilbert Blythe, and buried her face in her arms on the desk. Ruby Gillis, who got a glimpse of it as it went down, told the others going home from school that she'd 'acksually never seen anything like it – it was so white, with awful little red spots in it.'

To Anne, this was as the end of all things. It was bad enough to be singled out for punishment from among a dozen equally guilty ones; it was worse still to be sent to sit with a boy; but that that boy should be Gilbert Blythe was heaping insult on injury to a degree utterly unbearable. Anne felt that she could *not* bear it and it would be of no use to try. Her whole being seethed with shame and anger and humiliation.

At first the other scholars looked and whispered and giggled and nudged. But as Anne never lifted her head and as Gilbert worked fractions as if his whole soul was absorbed in them and them only, they soon returned to their own tasks and Anne was forgotten. When Mr Phillips called the history class out Anne should have gone; but Anne did not move, and Mr Phillips, who had been writing some verses 'To Priscilla' before he called the class, was thinking about an obstinate rhyme still and never missed her. Once, when nobody was looking, Gilbert took from his desk a little pink candy heart with a gold motto on it, 'You are sweet', and slipped it under the curve of Anne's arm. Whereupon Anne arose, took the pink heart gingerly between the tips of her fingers, dropped it on the floor, ground it to powder beneath her heel, and resumed her position without deigning to bestow a glance on Gilbert.

When school went out Anne marched to her desk, ostentatiously took out everything therein, books and writing tablet, pen and ink, testament and arithmetic, and piled them neatly on her cracked slate.

'What are you taking all those things home for, Anne?' Diana wanted to know, as soon as they were out on the road. She had not dared to ask the question before.

'I am not coming back to school any more,' said Anne.

Diana gasped and stared at Anne to see if she meant it.

'Will Marilla let you stay home?' she asked.

'She'll have to,' said Anne. 'I'll *never* go to school to that man again.'

'Oh, Anne!' Diana looked as if she were ready to cry. 'I do think you're mean. What shall I do? Mr Phillips will make me sit with that horrid Gertie Pye – I know he will, because she is sitting alone. Do come back, Anne.'

'I'd do almost anything in the world for you, Diana,' said Anne sadly. 'I'd let myself be torn limb from limb if it would do you any good. But I can't do this, so please don't ask it. You harrow up my very soul.'

'Just think of all the fun you will miss,' mourned Diana. 'We are going to build the loveliest new house down by the brook; and we'll be playing ball next week and you've never played ball, Anne. It's tremendously exciting. And we're going to learn a new song – Jane Andrews is practising it up now; and Alice Andrews is going to bring a new Pansy book next week and we're all going to read it out loud, chapter about, down by the brook. And you know you are so fond of reading out loud, Anne.'

Nothing moved Anne in the least. Her mind was made up. She would not go to school to Mr Phillips again; she told Marilla so when she got home.

'Nonsense,' said Marilla.

'It isn't nonsense at all,' said Anne, gazing at Marilla, with solemn, reproachful eyes. 'Don't you understand, Marilla? I've been insulted.'

'Insulted fiddlesticks! You'll go to school to-morrow as usual.'

'Oh, no.' Anne shook her head gently. 'I'm not going back, Marilla. I'll learn my lessons at home and

I'll be as good as I can be and hold my tongue all the time if it's possible at all. But I will not go back to school I assure you.'

Marilla saw something remarkably like unyielding stubbornness looking out of Anne's small face. She understood that she would have trouble in overcoming it; but she resolved wisely to say nothing more just then.

'I'll run down and see Rachel about it this evening,' she thought. 'There's no use reasoning with Anne now. She's too worked up and I've an idea she can be awful stubborn if she takes the notion. Far as I can make out from her story, Mr Phillips has been carrying matters with a rather high hand. But it would never do to say so to her. I'll just talk it over with Rachel. She's sent ten children to school and she ought to know something about it. She'll have heard the whole story, too, by this time.'

Marilla found Mrs Lynde knitting quilts as industriously and cheerfully as usual.

'I suppose you know what I've come about,' she said, a little shamefacedly.

Mrs Rachel nodded.

'About Anne's fuss in school, I reckon,' she said. 'Tillie Boulter was in on her way home from school and told me about it.'

'I don't know what to do with her,' said Marilla. 'She declares she won't go back to school. I never saw a child so worked up. I've been expecting trouble ever since she started to school. I knew things were going too smooth to last. She's so high-strung. What would you advise, Rachel?'

'Well, since you've asked my advice, Marilla,' said Mrs Lynde amiably – Mrs Lynde dearly loved to be asked for advice – 'I'd just humour her a little at first, that's what I'd do. It's my belief that Mr Phillips was in the wrong. Of course, it doesn't do to say so to the children, you know. And of course he did right to punish her yesterday for giving way to temper. But today it was different. The others who were late should have been punished as well as Anne, that's what. And I don't believe in making the girls sit with the boys for punishment. It isn't modest. Tillie Boulter was real indignant. She took Anne's part right through and said all the scholars did, too. Anne seems real popular among them, some-how. I never thought she'd take with them so well.'

'Then you really think I'd better let her stay home,' said Marilla in amazement.

'Yes. That is, I wouldn't say school to her again until she said it herself. Depend upon it, Marilla, she'll cool off in a week or so and be ready enough to go back of her own accord, that's what, while, if you were to make her go back right off, dear knows what freak or tantrum she'd take next and make more trouble than ever. The less fuss made the better, in my opinion. She won't miss much by not going to school, as far as *that* goes. Mr Phillips isn't any good at all as a teacher. The order he keeps is scandalous, that's what, and he neglects the young fry and puts all his time on those big scholars he's getting ready for Queen's. He'd never have got the school for another year if his uncle hadn't been a trustee – *the* trustee, for he just leads the other two around by the nose, that's what. I declare, I don't know what education in this Island is coming to.'

Mrs Rachel shook her head, as much as to say if she were only at the head of the educational system of the Province things would be much better managed.

Marilla took Mrs Rachel's advice and not another

word was said to Anne about going back to school. She learned her lessons at home, did her chores, and played with Diana in the chilly purple autumn twilights; but when she met Gilbert Blythe on the road or encountered him in Sunday-school she passed him by with an icy contempt that was no whit thawed by his evident desire to appease her. Even Diana's efforts as a peacemaker were of no avail. Anne had evidently made up her mind to hate Gilbert Blythe to the end of life.

As much as she hated Gilbert, however, did she love Diana, with all the love of her passionate little heart, equally intense in its likes and dislikes. One evening Marilla, coming in from the orchard with a basket of apples, found Anne sitting alone by the east window in the twilight, crying bitterly.

'Whatever's the matter now, Anne?' she asked.

'It's about Diana,' sobbed Anne luxuriously. 'I love Diana so, Marilla. I cannot ever live without her. But I know very well when we grow up that Diana will get married and go away and leave me. And oh, what shall I do? I hate her husband — I just hate him furiously. I've been imagining it all out — the wedding and everything — Diana dressed in snowy garments, 25 with a veil, and looking as beautiful and regal as a queen; and me the bridesmaid, with a lovely dress, too, and puffed sleeves, but with a breaking heart hid beneath my smiling face. And then bidding Diana good-bye-e-e –' Here Anne broke down entirely and wept with increasing bitterness.

Marilla turned quickly away to hide her twitching face; but it was no use; she collapsed on the nearest chair and burst into such a hearty and unusual peal of laughter that Matthew, crossing the yard outside, halted in amazement. When had he heard Marilla laugh like that before?

'Well, Anne Shirley,' said Marilla as soon as she could speak, 'if you must borrow trouble, for pity's sake borrow it handier home. I should think you had an imagination, sure enough.'

Diana is Invited to Tea,
with Tragic Results

OCTOBER was a beautiful month at Green Gables, when the birches in the hollow turned as golden as sunshine and the maples behind the orchard were royal crimson and the wild cherry-trees along the lane put on the loveliest shades of dark red and bronzy green, while the fields sunned themselves in aftermaths.

Anne revelled in the world of colour about her.

'Oh, Marilla,' she exclaimed one Saturday morning, coming dancing in with her arms full of gorgeous boughs, 'I'm so glad I live in a world where there are Octobers. It would be terrible if we just skipped from September to November, wouldn't it? Look at these maple branches. Don't they give you a thrill – several thrills? I'm going to decorate my room with them.'

'Messy things,' said Marilla, whose aesthetic sense was not noticeably developed. 'You clutter up your room entirely too much with out-of-doors stuff, Anne. Bedrooms were made to sleep in.'

'Oh, and dream in, too, Marilla. And you know one can dream so much better in a room where there are pretty things. I'm going to put these boughs in the old blue jug and set them on my table.'

'Mind you don't drop leaves all over the stairs then. I'm going to a meeting of the Aid Society at Carmody this afternoon, Anne, and I won't likely be home before dark. You'll have to get Matthew and Jerry their supper, so mind you don't forget to put the tea to draw until you sit down at the table as you did last time.'

'It was dreadful of me to forget,' said Anne apologetically, 'but that was the afternoon I was trying to think of a name for Violet Vale and it crowded other things out. Matthew was so good. He never scolded a bit. He put the tea down himself and said we could wait awhile as well as not. And I told him a lovely fairy story while we were waiting, so he didn't find the time long at all. It was a beautiful fairy story, Marilla. I forgot the end of it, so I made up an end for it myself and Matthew said he couldn't tell where the join came in.'

'Matthew would think it all right, Anne, if you took a notion to get up and have dinner in the middle of the night. But you keep your wits about you this time. And – I don't really know if I'm doing right – it may make you more addle-pated than ever – but you can ask Diana to come over and spend the afternoon with you and have tea here.'

'Oh, Marilla!' Anne clasped her hands. 'How perfectly lovely! You *are* able to imagine things after all or else you'd never have understood how I've longed for that very thing. It will seem so nice and grown-uppish. No fear of my forgetting to put the tea to draw when I have company. Oh, Marilla, can I use the rosebud spray tea-set?'

'No, indeed! The rosebud tea-set! Well, what next? You know I never use that except for the minister or the Aids. You'll put down the old brown tea-set. But you can open the little yellow crock of cherry preserves. It's time it was being used anyhow – I believe it's beginning to go. And you can cut some fruit-cake and have some of the cookies and snaps.'

'I can just imagine myself sitting down at the head of the table and pouring out the tea,' said Anne, shutting her eyes ecstatically. 'And asking Diana if she takes sugar! I know she doesn't, but of course I'll ask her just as if I didn't know. And then pressing her to take another piece of fruit-cake and another helping of preserves. Oh, Marilla, it's a wonderful sensation just to think of it. Can I take her into the spare room to lay off her hat when she comes? And then into the parlour to sit?'

'No. The sitting-room will do for you and your company. But there's a bottle half-full of raspberry cordial that was left over from the church social the other night. It's on the second shelf of the sitting-room closet and you and Diana can have it if you like, and a cooky to eat with it along in the afternoon, for I dare say Matthew'll be late coming in to tea since he's hauling potatoes to the vessel.'

Anne fled down to the hollow, past the Dryad's Bubble and up the spruce path to Orchard Slope, to ask Diana to tea. As a result, just after Marilla had driven off to Carmody, Diana came over, dressed in her second best dress and looking exactly as it is proper to look when asked out to tea. At other times she was wont to run into the kitchen without knocking; but now she knocked primly at the front door. And when Anne, dressed in *her* second best, as primly

opened it, both little girls shook hands as gravely as if

they had never met before. This unnatural solemnity lasted until after Diana had been taken to the east gable to lay off her hat and then had sat for ten minutes in the sitting-room, toes in position.

'How is your mother?' inquired Anne politely just as if she had not seen Mrs Barry picking apples that morning in excellent health and spirits.

'She is very well, thank you. I suppose Mr Cuthbert is hauling potatoes to the *Lily Sands* this afternoon, is he?' said Diana, who had ridden down to Mr Harmon Andrews's that morning in Matthew's cart.

'Yes. Our potato crop is very good this year. I hope your father's potato crop is good, too.'

'It is fairly good, thank you. Have you picked many of your apples yet?'

'Oh, ever so many,' said Anne, forgetting to be dignified and jumping up quickly. 'Let's go out to the orchard and get some of the Red Sweetings, Diana. Marilla says we can have all that are left on the tree. Marilla is a very generous woman. She said we could have fruit-cake and cherry preserves for tea. But it isn't good manners to tell your company what you are going to give them to eat, so I won't tell you what she said we could have to drink. Only it begins 31 with an *r* and a *c* and it's a bright red colour. I love bright red drinks, don't you? They taste twice as good as any other colour.'

The orchard, with its great sweeping boughs that bent to the ground with fruit, proved so delightful that the little girls spent most of the afternoon in it, sitting in a grassy corner where the frost had spared the green and the mellow autumn sunshine lingered warmly, eating apples and talking as hard as they could. Diana had much to tell Anne of what went on in school. She had to sit with Gertie Pye and she hated it; Gertie squeaked her pencil all the time and it just made her – Diana's – blood run cold; Ruby Gillis had charmed all her warts away, true's you live, with a magic pebble that old Mary Joe from the Creek gave her. You had to rub the warts with the pebble and then throw it away over your left shoulder at the time of the new moon and the warts would all go. Charlie Sloane's name was written up with Em White's on the porch wall and Em White was *awful mad* about it; Sam Boulter had 'sassed' Mr Phillips in class and Mr Phillips whipped him and Sam's father came down to the school and dared Mr Phillips to lay a hand on one of his children again;

and Mattie Andrews had a new red hood and a blue crossover with tassels on it, and the airs she put on about it were perfectly sickening; and Lizzie Wright didn't speak to Mamie Wilson because Mamie Wilson's grown-up sister had cut out Lizzie Wright's grown-up sister with her beau; and everybody missed Anne so and wished she'd come to school again; and Gilbert Blythe –

But Anne didn't want to hear about Gilbert Blythe. She jumped up hurriedly and said suppose they go in and have some raspberry cordial.

Anne looked on the second shelf of the room pantry, but there was no bottle of raspberry cordial there. Search revealed it away back on the top shelf. Anne put it on a tray and set it on the table with a tumbler.

'Now, please help yourself, Diana,' she said politely. 'I don't believe I'll have any just now. I don't feel as if I wanted any after all those apples.'

Diana poured herself out a tumblerful, looked at its bright red hue admiringly, and then sipped it daintily.

'That's awfully nice raspberry cordial, Anne,' she said. 'I didn't know raspberry cordial was so nice.'

'I'm real glad you like it. Take as much as you want. I'm going to run out and stir the fire up. There are so many responsibilities on a person's mind when they're keeping house, isn't there?'

When Anne came back from the kitchen Diana was drinking her second glassful of cordial; and, being entreated thereto by Anne, she offered no particular objection to the drinking of a third. The tumblerfuls were generous ones and the raspberry cordial was certainly very nice.

'The nicest I ever drank,' said Diana. 'It's ever so much nicer than Mrs Lynde's although she brags of hers so much. It doesn't taste a bit like hers.'

'I should think Marilla's raspberry cordial would prob'ly be much nicer than Mrs Lynde's,' said Anne loyally. 'Marilla is a famous cook. She is trying to teach me to cook, but I assure you, Diana, it is uphill work. There's so little scope for imagination in cookery. You just have to go by rules. The last time I made a cake I forgot to put the flour in. I was thinking the loveliest story about you and me, Diana. I thought you were desperately ill with smallpox and everybody deserted you, but I went boldly to your bedside and nursed you back to life; and then I took the smallpox and died and I was buried under those poplar-trees in the graveyard and you planted a rose-bush by my grave and watered it with your tears; and you never, never forgot the friend of your youth who sacrificed her life for you. Oh, it was such a pathetic little tale, Diana. The tears just rained down over my cheeks while I mixed the cake. But I forgot the flour and the cake was a dismal failure. Flour is so essential to cakes, you know. Marilla was very cross and I don't wonder. I'm a great trial to her. She was terribly mortified about the pudding sauce last week. We had a plum pudding for dinner on Tuesday and there was half the pudding and a pitcherful of sauce left over. Marilla said there was enough for another dinner and told me to set it on the pantry shelf and cover it. I meant to cover it just as much as could be, Diana, but when I carried it in I was imagining I was a nun – of course I'm a Protestant, but I imagined I was a Catholic – taking the veil to bury a broken heart in cloistered seclusion; and I forgot all about covering the pudding sauce. I thought of it next morning and ran to the pantry. Diana, fancy if you can my extreme horror at finding a mouse drowned in that pudding sauce! I lifted the mouse out with a spoon and threw it out in the yard and then I washed the spoon in three waters. Marilla was out milking and I fully intended to ask her when she came in if I'd give the sauce to the pigs; but when she did come in I was imagining that I was a frost-fairy going through the woods turning the trees red and yellow, whichever they wanted to be, so I never thought about the pudding sauce again and Marilla sent me out to pick apples. Well, Mr and Mrs Chester Ross from Spencervale came here that morning. You know they are very stylish people, especially Mrs Chester Ross. When Marilla called me in, dinner was all ready and everybody was at the table. I tried to be as polite and dignified as I could be, for I wanted Mrs Chester Ross to think I was a ladylike little girl even if I wasn't pretty. Everything went right until I saw Marilla coming with the plum pudding in one hand and the pitcher of pudding sauce, *warmed up*, in the other. Diana, that was a terrible moment. I remembered everything and I just stood up in my place and shrieked out, "Marilla, you mustn't use that pudding sauce. There was a mouse drowned in it. I forgot to tell you before." Oh, Diana, I shall never forget that awful moment if I live to be a hundred. Mrs Chester

Ross just *looked* at me and I thought I would sink through the floor with mortification. She is such a perfect housekeeper and fancy what she must have thought of us. Marilla turned red as fire but she never said a word – then. She just carried that sauce and pudding out and brought in some strawberry preserves. She even offered me some, but I couldn't swallow a mouthful. It was like heaping coals of fire on my head. After Mrs Chester Ross went away Marilla gave me a dreadful scolding. Why, Diana, what is the matter?'

Diana had stood up very unsteadily; then she sat down again, putting her hands to her head.

'I'm – I'm awful sick,' she said, a little thickly. 'I – I – must go right home.'

'Oh, you mustn't dream of going home without your tea,' cried Anne in distress. 'I'll get it right off – I'll go and put the tea down this very minute.'

'I must go home,' repeated Diana, stupidly but determinedly.

'Let me get you a lunch anyhow,' implored Anne. 'Let me give you a bit of fruit-cake and some of the cherry preserves. Lie down on the sofa for a little while and you'll be better. Where do you feel bad?'

'I must go home,' said Diana, and that was all she would say. In vain Anne pleaded.

'I never heard of company going home without tea,' she mourned. 'Oh, Diana, do you suppose that it's possible you're really taking the smallpox? If you are I'll go and nurse you, you can depend on that. I'll never forsake you. But I do wish you'd stay till after tea. Where do you feel bad?'

'I'm awful dizzy,' said Diana.

And, indeed, she walked very dizzily. Anne, with tears of disappointment in her eyes, got Diana's hat and went with her as far as the Barry yard fence. Then she wept all the way back to Green Gables, where she sorrowfully put the remainder of the raspberry cordial back into the pantry and got tea ready for Matthew and Jerry, with all the zest gone out of the performance.

The next day was Sunday and as the rain poured down in torrents from dawn till dusk, Anne did not stir abroad from Green Gables. Monday afternoon Marilla sent her down to Mrs Lynde's on an errand. In a very short space of time Anne came flying back up the lane, with tears rolling down her cheeks. Into the kitchen she dashed and flung herself face downwards on the sofa in an agony.

38

'Whatever has gone wrong now, Anne?' queried Marilla in doubt and dismay. 'I do hope you haven't gone and been saucy to Mrs Lynde again.'

No answer from Anne save more tears and stormier sobs!

'Anne Shirley, when I ask you a question I want to be answered. Sit right up this very minute and tell me what you are crying about.'

Anne sat up, tragedy personified.

'Mrs Lynde was up to see Mrs Barry today and Mrs Barry was in an awful state,' she wailed. 'She says that I set Diana *drunk* Saturday and sent her home in a disgraceful condition. And she says I must be a thoroughly bad, wicked little girl and she's never, never going to let Diana play with me again. Oh, Marilla, I'm just overcome with woe.'

Marilla stared in blank amazement.

'Set Diana drunk!' she said when she found her voice. 'Anne, are you or Mrs Barry crazy? What on earth did you give her?'

'Not a thing but raspberry cordial,' sobbed Anne. 'I never thought raspberry cordial would set people drunk, Marilla — not even if they drank three big tumblerfuls as Diana did. Oh, it sounds so — so — like

Mrs Thomas's husband! But I didn't mean to set her drunk.'

'Drunk fiddlesticks!' said Marilla, marching to the sitting-room pantry. There on the shelf was a bottle which she at once recognized as one containing some of her three-year-old home-made currant wine, for which she was celebrated in Avonlea, although certain of the stricter sort, Mrs Barry among them, disapproved strongly of it. And at the same time Marilla recollected that she had put the bottle of raspberry cordial down in the cellar instead of in the pantry as she had told Anne.

She went back to the kitchen with the wine bottle in her hand. Her face was twitching in spite of herself.

'Anne, you certainly have a genius for getting into trouble. You went and gave Diana currant wine instead of raspberry cordial. Didn't you know the difference yourself?'

'I never tasted it,' said Anne. 'I thought it was the cordial. I meant to be so – so – hospitable. Diana got awfully sick and had to go home. Mrs Barry told Mrs Lynde she was simply dead drunk. She just laughed silly-like when her mother asked her what was the matter and went to sleep and slept for hours. Her mother smelled her breath and knew she was drunk. She had a fearful headache all day yesterday. Mrs Barry is so indignant. She will never believe but what I did it on purpose.'

'I should think she would better punish Diana for being so greedy as to drink three glassfuls of anything,' said Marilla shortly. 'Why, three of those big glasses would have made her sick even if it had only been cordial. Well, this story will be a nice handle for those folks who are so down on me for making currant wine, although I haven't made any for three years ever since I found out that the minister didn't approve. I just kept that bottle for sickness. There, there, child, don't cry. I can't see as you were to blame although I'm sorry it happened so.'

'I must cry,' said Anne. 'My heart is broken. The stars in their courses fight against me, Marilla. Diana and I are parted for ever. Oh, Marilla, I little dreamed of this when first we swore our vows of friendship.'

'Don't be foolish, Anne. Mrs Barry will think better of it when she finds you're not really to blame. I suppose she thinks you've done it for a silly joke or something of that sort. You'd best go up this evening and tell her how it was.'

'My courage fails me at the thought of facing Diana's injured mother,' sighed Anne. 'I wish you'd go, Marilla. You're so much more dignified than I am. Likely she'd listen to you quicker than to me.'

'Well, I will,' said Marilla, reflecting that it would probably be the wiser course. 'Don't cry any more, Anne. It will be all right.'

Marilla had changed her mind about its being all right by the time she got back from Orchard Slope. Anne was watching for her coming and flew to the porch door to meet her.

'Oh, Marilla, I know by your face that it's been no use,' she said sorrowfully. 'Mrs Barry won't forgive me?'

'Mrs Barry, indeed!' snapped Marilla. 'Of all the unreasonable women I ever saw she's the worst. I told her it was all a mistake and you weren't to blame, but she just simply didn't believe me. And she rubbed it well in about my currant wine and how I'd always said it couldn't have the least effect on anybody. I just told her plainly that currant wine wasn't meant to be drunk three tumblerfuls at a time and that if a child I had to do with was so greedy I'd sober her up with a right good spanking.'

Marilla whisked into the kitchen, grievously disturbed, leaving a very much distracted little soul in the porch behind her. Presently Anne stepped out bare-headed into the chill autumn dusk; very determinedly and steadily she took her way down through the sere clover field over the log bridge and up through the spruce grove, lighted by a pale little moon hanging low over the western woods. Mrs Barry, coming to the door in answer to a timid knock, found a white-lipped, eager-eyed suppliant on the doorstep.

Her face hardened. Mrs Barry was a woman of strong prejudices and dislikes, and her anger was of the cold, sullen sort which is always hardest to overcome. To do her justice, she really believed Anne had made Diana drunk out of sheer malice prepense, and she was honestly anxious to preserve her little daughter from the contamination of further intimacy with such a child.

'What do you want?' she said stiffly.

Anne clasped her hands.

'Oh, Mrs Barry, please forgive me. I did not mean 43

to – to – intoxicate Diana. How could I? Just imagine if you were a poor little orphan girl that kind people had adopted and you had just one bosom friend in all the world. Do you think you would intoxicate her on purpose? I thought it was only raspberry cordial. I was firmly convinced it was raspberry cordial. Oh, please don't say that you won't let Diana play with me any more. If you do you will cover my life with a dark cloud of woe.'

This speech, which would have softened good Mrs Lynde's heart in a twinkling, had no effect on Mrs Barry except to irritate her still more. She was suspicious of Anne's big words and dramatic gestures and imagined that the child was making fun of her. So she said, coldly and cruelly:

'I don't think you are a fit little girl for Diana to associate with. You'd better go home and behave yourself.'

Anne's lip quivered.

'Won't you let me see Diana just once to say fare-well?' she implored.

'Diana has gone over to Carmody with her father,' said Mrs Barry, going in and shutting the door.

Anne went back to Green Gables calm with despair.

'My last hope is gone,' she told Marilla. 'I went up and saw Mrs Barry myself and she treated me very insultingly. Marilla, I do *not* think she is a well-bred woman. There is nothing more to do except to pray and I haven't much hope that that'll do much good because, Marilla, I do not believe that God Himself can do very much with such an obstinate person as Mrs Barry.'

'Anne, you shouldn't say such things,' rebuked Marilla, striving to overcome that unholy tendency to laughter which she was dismayed to find growing upon her. And indeed, when she told the whole story to Matthew that night, she did laugh heartily over Anne's tribulations.

But when she slipped into the east gable before going to bed and found that Anne had cried herself to sleep an unaccustomed softness crept into her face.

'Poor little soul,' she murmured, lifting a loose curl of hair from the child's tear-stained face. Then she bent down and kissed the flushed cheek on the pillow.

A New Interest in Life

THE next afternoon Anne, bending over her patchwork at the kitchen window, happened to glance out and beheld Diana down by the Dryad's Bubble beckoning mysteriously. In a trice Anne was out of the house and flying down to the hollow, astonishment and hope struggling in her expressive eyes. But the hope faded when she saw Diana's dejected countenance.

'Your mother hasn't relented?' she gasped.

Diana shook her head mournfully.

'No; and oh, Anne, she says I'm never to play with you again. I've cried and cried and I told her it wasn't your fault, but it wasn't any use. I had ever such a time coaxing her to let me come down and say good-bye to you. She said I was only to stay ten minutes and she's timing me by the clock.'

'Ten minutes isn't very long to say an eternal farewell in,' said Anne tearfully. 'Oh, Diana, will you promise faithfully never to forget me, the friend of your youth, no matter what dearer friends may caress thee?'

'Indeed I will,' sobbed Diana, 'and I'll never have another bosom friend – I don't want to have. I couldn't love anybody as I love you.'

'Oh, Diana,' cried Anne, clasping her hands, 'do you *love* me?'

'Why, of course I do. Didn't you know that?'

'No.' Anne drew a long breath. 'I thought you *liked* me, of course, but I never hoped you *loved* me. Why, Diana, I didn't think anybody could love me. Nobody ever has loved me since I can remember. Oh, this is wonderful! It's a ray of light which will for ever shine on the darkness of a path severed from thee, Diana. Oh, just say it once again.'

'I love you devotedly, Anne,' said Diana staunchly, 'and I always will, you may be sure of that.'

'And I will always love thee, Diana,' said Anne, solemnly extending her hand. 'In the years to come thy memory will shine like a star over my lonely life, as that last story we read together says. Diana, wilt thou give me a lock of thy jet-black tresses in parting to treasure for evermore?'

'Have you got anything to cut it with?' queried Diana, wiping away the tears which Anne's affecting accents had caused to flow afresh, and returning to practicalities.

'Yes. I've got my patchwork scissors in my apron pocket fortunately,' said Anne. She solemnly clipped one of Diana's curls. 'Fare thee well, my beloved friend. Henceforth we must be as strangers though living side by side. But my heart will ever be faithful to thee.'

Anne stood and watched Diana out of sight, mournfully waving her hand to the latter whenever she turned to look back. Then she returned to the house, not a little consoled for the time being by this romantic parting.

'It is all over,' she informed Marilla. 'I shall never have another friend. I'm really worse off than ever before, for I haven't Katie Maurice and Violetta now. And even if I had it wouldn't be the same. Somehow, little dream girls are not satisfying after a real friend. Diana and I had such an affecting farewell down by the spring. It will be sacred in my memory for ever. I used the most pathetic language I could think of and said "thou" and "thee". "Thou" and "thee" seems so much more romantic than "you". Diana gave me a lock of her hair and I'm going to sew it up in a little bag and wear it around my neck all my life. Please see that it is buried with me, for I don't believe I'll live very long. Perhaps when she sees me lying cold and dead before her Mrs Barry may feel remorse for what she has done and will let Diana come to my funeral.'

'I don't think there is much fear of your dying of grief as long as you can talk, Anne,' said Marilla unsympathetically.

The following Monday Anne surprised Marilla by coming down from her room with her basket of books on her arm and her lips primmed up into a line of determination.

'I'm going back to school,' she announced. 'That is all there is left in life for me, now that my friend has been ruthlessly torn from me. In school I can look at her and muse over days departed.'

'You'd better muse over your lessons and sums,' said Marilla, concealing her delight at this development of the situation. 'If you're going back to school I hope we'll hear no more of breaking slates over people's heads and such carryings-on. Behave yourself and do just what your teacher tells you.'

'I'll try to be a model pupil,' agreed Anne

dolefully. 'There won't be much fun in it, I expect. Mr Phillips said Minnie Andrews was a model pupil and there isn't a spark of imagination or life in her. She is just dull and poky and never seems to have a good time. But I feel so depressed that perhaps it will come easy to me now. I'm going round by the road. I couldn't bear to go by the Birch Path all alone. I should weep bitter tears if I did.'

Anne was welcomed back to school with open arms. Her imagination had been sorely missed in games, her voice in the singing, and her dramatic ability in the perusal aloud of books at dinner hour. Ruby Gillis smuggled three blue plums over to her during testament reading; Ella May Macpherson gave her an enormous yellow pansy cut from the covers of a floral catalogue – a species of desk decoration much prized in Avonlea school. Sophia Sloane offered to teach her a perfectly elegant new pattern of knit lace, *so* nice for trimming aprons. Katie Boulter gave her a perfume bottle to keep slate-water in, and Julia Bell copied carefully on a piece of pale pink paper, scalloped on the edges, the following effusion:

TO ANNE
When twilight drops her curtain down
And pins it with a star
Remember that you have a friend
Though she may wander far.

'It's so nice to be appreciated,' sighed Anne rapturously to Marilla that night.

The girls were not the only scholars who 'appreciated' her. When Anne went to her seat after dinner hour – she had been told by Mr Phillips to sit with the model Minnie Andrews – she found on her desk a big, luscious 'strawberry apple'. Anne caught it up all ready to take a bite, when she remembered that the only place in Avonlea where strawberry apples grew was in the old Blythe orchard on the other side of the Lake of Shining Waters. Anne dropped the apple as if it were a red-hot coal and ostentatiously wiped her fingers on her handkerchief. The apple lay untouched on her desk until the next morning, when little Timothy Andrews, who swept the school and kindled the fire, annexed it as one of his perquisites. Charlie Sloane's slate pencil, gorgeously bedizened with striped red and yellow paper, costing two cents where ordinary pencils cost only one, which he sent up to her after dinner hour, met with a more favourable reception. Anne was graciously pleased to accept it and rewarded the donor with a smile which exalted that infatuated youth straightway into the seventh heaven of delight and caused him to make such fearful errors in his dictation that Mr Phillips kept him in after school to rewrite it.

But as

> The Caesar's pageant shorn of Brutus' bust
> Did but of Rome's best son remind her more,

so the marked absence of any tribute or recognition from Diana Barry, who was sitting with Gertie Pye, embittered Anne's little triumph.

'Diana might just have smiled at me once, I think,' she mourned to Marilla that night. But the next morning a note, most fearfully and wonderfully twisted and folded, and a small parcel, were passed across to Anne.

Dear Anne [ran the former],

Mother says I'm not to play with you or talk to you even in school. It isn't my fault and don't be cross at me, because I love you as much as ever. I miss you awfully to tell all my secrets to and I don't like Gertie Pye one bit. I made you one of the new bookmarkers out of red tissue paper. They are awfully fashionable now and only three girls in school know how to make them. When you look at it remember

Your true friend,
DIANA BARRY

Anne read the note, kissed the bookmark, and dispatched a prompt reply back to the other side of the school.

My own darling Diana,

Of course I am not cross at you because you have to obey your mother. Our spirits can commune. I shall keep your lovely present for ever. Minnie Andrews is a very nice little girl – although she has no imagination – but after having been Diana's busum friend I cannot be Minnie's. Please excuse mistakes because my spelling isn't very good yet, although much improved.

Yours until death do us part,
ANNE or CORDELIA SHIRLEY

P.S. I shall sleep with your letter under my pillow tonight.
A. or C.S.

Marilla pessimistically expected more trouble since Anne had again begun to go to school. But none developed. Perhaps Anne caught something of the 'model' spirit from Minnie Andrews; at least she got on very well with Mr Phillips thenceforth. She flung herself into her studies heart and soul, determined not to be out-done in any class by Gilbert Blythe. The rivalry between them was soon apparent; it was entirely good-natured on Gilbert's side; but it is much to be feared that the same thing cannot be said of Anne, who had certainly an unpraiseworthy tenacity for holding grudges. She was as intense in her hatreds as in her loves. She would not stoop to admit that she meant to rival Gilbert in school work, because that would have been to acknowledge his existence which Anne persistently ignored; but the rivalry was there and honours fluctuated between them. Now Gilbert was head of the spelling class; now Anne, with a toss of her long red braids, spelled him down. One morning Gilbert had all his sums done correctly and had his name written on the blackboard on the roll of honour; the next morning Anne, having wrestled wildly with decimals the entire evening before, would be first. One awful day they were ties and their names were written up together. It was almost as bad as a 'take-notice', and Anne's mortification was as evident as Gilbert's satisfaction. When the written examinations at the end of each month were held the suspense was terrible. The first month Gilbert came out three marks ahead. The second Anne beat him by five. But her triumph was marred by the fact that Gilbert congratulated her heartily before the whole school. It would have been ever so much sweeter to her if he had felt the sting of his defeat.

Mr Phillips might not be a very good teacher; but a pupil so inflexibly determined on learning as Anne was could hardly escape making progress under any kind of a teacher. By the end of the term Anne and Gilbert were both promoted into the fifth class and allowed to begin studying the elements of 'the branches' – by which Latin, geometry, French, and algebra were meant. In geometry Anne met her Waterloo.

'It's perfectly awful stuff, Marilla,' she groaned. 'I'm sure I'll never be able to make head or tail of it. There is no scope for imagination in it at all. Mr Phillips says I'm the worst dunce he ever saw at it.

And Gil – I mean some of the others are so smart at it. It is extremely mortifying, Marilla. Even Diana gets along better than I do. But I don't mind being beaten by Diana. Even although we meet as strangers now I still love her with an *inextinguishable* love. It makes me very sad at times to think about her. But really, Marilla, one can't stay sad very long in such an interesting world, can one?'

Some Puffin books by L. M. Montgomery

(in reading order)

ANNE OF GREEN GABLES
ANNE OF AVONLEA
ANNE OF THE ISLAND
ANNE OF WINDY WILLOWS
ANNE'S HOUSE OF DREAMS
ANNE OF INGLESIDE
RAINBOW VALLEY
RILLA OF INGLESIDE

CHRONICLES OF AVONLEA
FURTHER CHRONICLES OF AVONLEA

EMILY OF NEW MOON
EMILY CLIMBS